# DOCTOR WHO

## THE ULTIMATE QUIZ BOOK

Jack Goldstein

&

Paul Andrews

ACORN BOOKS
WWW.ACORNBOOKS.CO.UK

Published in 2016 by
Acorn Books
www.acornbooks.co.uk

Acorn Books is an imprint of
Andrews UK Limited
www.andrewsuk.com

# Contents

| | QUESTIONS | ANSWERS |
|---|---|---|

# Introduction

We won't keep you long, as you're bound to want to dive straight into the quiz. So all we'd like to do in this brief introduction is to explain a couple of 'rules' we stuck to when writing the quiz. Firstly, we use the words *story*, *serial* and *episode* rather interchangeably; however as a general pointer, *episode* refers to 'new Who' (i.e. from the ninth Doctor onwards), whereas *serial* refers to the first 'batch' of Doctors. *Story* essentially means *either* an episode *or* serial. *Companion* generally refers to a Doctor's sidekick who has travelled in the TARDIS with him. *Monster* usually means any alien race encountered, and in this quiz they are mostly – but not always – enemies. Hopefully that clarifies things for you... and all but the most pedantic fan should be able to figure most of this out as they go. Good luck and have fun!

# The Quiz

# The Questions

# Stories – Which Doctor? [1]

*Which Doctor (first to twelfth) took the lead in the following serials or episodes..?*

1. *Army of Ghosts*

2. *The Celestial Toymaker*

3. *The Krotons*

4. *Death to the Daleks*

5. *The Pirate Planet*

6. *Cold War*

7. *Earthshock*

8. *The Faceless Ones*

9. *The Edge of Destruction*

10. *Night Terrors*

# Monsters – Which Doctor? (1)

*Which Doctor (first to twelfth) first came across these monsters..?*

11.  Fenric

12.  Zocci

13.  Dalek

14.  Isolus

15.  Ood

16.  The Wire

17.  Tractator

18.  Giant Maggots

19.  Toclafane

20.  Sycorax

# Monsters – Which Story? (1)

*In which story (serial or episode) are we first introduced to these monsters..?*

21.  Mandrel

22.  Vanir

23.  The Fisher King

24.  Cryon

25.  Atraxi

26.  Auton

27.  The Silence

28.  Great Intelligence

29.  Draconian

30.  Time Zombie

# Pot Luck (1)

*Now a pot luck round, where the questions can be about anything...*

31. What race of creatures chopped off the Doctor's hand?

32. What was the accepted name of the vehicle the Third Doctor used which could fly?

33. What was the name of the companion who only travelled with the seventh Doctor?

34. What is the planet of the spiders called?

35. What unaired episode of the show was written by Douglas Adams?

36. Complete the title of this serial: *The Curse of F —*

37. Name all the actors to have played the Doctor *as a lead* on TV to date...

38. Which creatures face the second Doctor in the episode *The Invasion*?

39. What was the Doctor's robot dog called?

40. Which creatures 'take' Amy and Rory in their last episode?

# Planets (1)

*Which planets are being described here..?*

41. A rocky, barren planet covered by boulders, boulders and more boulders.

42. A lush, green planet also known as *The Garden Planet*.

43. Home planet of the mercenary Lytton.

44. Where the Graff Vynda-K's men fought in the Alliance Wars.

45. The planet Max Capricorn planned to retire to, which has ladies who are "very fond of... metal"

46. A planet where fiction is banned. It is also known as Colony World 4378976, Delta Four, Oneiros, Journey's End and Discovery.

47. This planet is said to have diamond coral reefs.

48. A planet with intelligent sand and singing fish.

49. Source of the rare ore zeiton-7.

50. The only planet, apart from Bandraginus V, on which the mineral Oolion occurs naturally.

# Anagram Companions (1)

*These are anagrams of some of the Doctor's companions. Can you figure out who they are..?*

51.  Benson Jack

52.  Whiz Sal

53.  Torn Jag

54.  La Eel

55.  A Manor

56.  Acrid

57.  Say S N

58.  Mad Pony

59.  Cea

60.  Brew or Nip

# Stories – Which Doctor? (2)

*Again, which Doctor took the lead in these stories..?*

61. *The Daleks' Master Plan*

62. *The Aztecs*

63. *Mindwarp*

64. *Pyramids of Mars*

65. *Colony in Space*

66. *Bad Wolf*

67. *The Unicorn and the Wasp*

68. *The Wheel in Space*

69. *Resurrection of the Daleks*

70. *Galaxy 4*

# Monsters – Which Doctor? (2)

*Another chance to say which doctor first encountered these foes...*

71. Raxacoricofallapatorian

72. Zarbi

73. Adipose

74. Peg Doll

75. Vanir

76. Tivolians

77. Draconian

78. Cryon

79. Pipe People

80. Carrionite

# Pot Luch (2)

*More general questions for you...*

81. What secret organisation does Captain Jack lead?

82. What is the name given to the Time Lord who tries to interfere with the first Doctor?

83. What creatures were discovered by the Doctor in the caves under Wenley Moor?

84. How many times is it generally accepted a Time Lord can regenerate?

85. What was Doctor's granddaughter called?

86. Which companion shared the same name as a playing card?

87. In what kind of surroundings in London did we see the TARDIS for the first time?

88. Which companion of the first Doctor shares their name with an extinct creature?

89. What organisation was the Brigadier in charge of?

90. Which actress plays River Song?

# Characters [1]

*To whom are we referring below..?*

91. The director and CEO of Torchwood One.

92. If this character loses a game, his world is destroyed (although he is powerful enough to rebuild it). If a contestant loses, they are added to the game as a toy.

93. This malevolent supercomputer resides in the Post Office Tower in London.

94. The ruthless leader of the Space Pirates.

95. A member of the Prydonian Chapter, a former teacher of the Doctor.

96. The designer of Paradise Towers and Miracle City.

97. An eccentric millionaire with an obsession for botany.

98. The chief of the Carion race.

99. A Neo-Nazi, based in South America, who aims to establish a Fourth Reich, aided by a powerful Time Lord weapon, known as the Nemesis.

100. Ruler of a human colony on Terra Alpha.

# Monster Anagrams (1)

*Here are some anagrams of monsters encountered throughout the show's history. Can you unscramble them?*

101. Resin

102. Arm Lend

103. Air Tax

104. A Runt

105. Nu Oat

106. Ape Swim

107. Crony

108. Halt

109. Cry Men Be

110. Scary Ox

# Who Played? (1)

*Which actor or actress played the following companions..?*

111.   Sergeant John Benton

112.   Sarah Jane Smith

113.   Zoe Heriot

114.   Rory Williams

115.   Donna Noble

116.   Steven Taylor

117.   Peri Brown

118.   Captain Mike Yates

119.   Rose Tyler

120.   Jo Grant

# Monsters – Which Story? (2)

*Again, in which story do we first find these aliens..?*

121. Krillitane

122. Tractator

123. The Veil

124. Gelth

125. Sisterhood of Karn

126. Logopolitan

127. Pipe People

128. Whisper Men

129. Zarbi

130. Vigil

# Pot Luck (3)

*More randomly selected questions...*

131. Under the city of 'New New York', what menace lurked?

132. What is the home planet of the Daleks called?

133. Which companion actor went on to be a *Blue Peter* presenter?

134. What is the device that is supposed to change the appearance of the Tardis called?

135. How many Doctors should have met up on the Death Zone?

136. What is the home planet of the Slitheen called?

137. What is the name of the Doctor's Time Lord nemesis?

138. What is the name of the episode in which – for the first time – it was revealed that Daleks could travel up stairs?

139. What is the surname of Jo, companion to the third Doctor?

140. Which famous Dutch painter did the Doctor meet?

# Which Doctor

*An easy round for most fans: which Doctor (from first to twelfth) was played by these actors..?*

141. William Hartnell

142. Christopher Eccleston

143. Jon Pertwee

144. Peter Davidson

145. David Tennant

146. Paul McGann

147. Colin Baker

148. Patrick Troughton

149. Tom Baker

150. Sylvester McCoy

# Companions (1)

*Of which Doctor were the following characters first companions?*

151. Tegan Jovanka

152. Grace Holloway

153. Susan Foreman

154. Rory Williams

155. Rose Tyler

156. Mickey Smith

157. Ian Chesterton

158. Melanie Bush

159. Jo Grant

160. K-9

# Stories – Which Doctor? (3)

*Time for more serials and episodes; which Doctor starred in these..?*

161. *The Savages*

162. *The Impossible Astronaut*

163. *The Stolen Earth*

164. *The Deadly Assassin*

165. *The Tomb of the Cybermen*

166. *Carnival of Monsters*

167. *An Unearthly Child*

168. *Paradise Towers*

169. *Planet of Giants*

170. *Genesis of the Daleks*

# Pot Luck (4)

*Time for more pot luck...*

171. What is the name of the shape-changing robot which travels with the Doctor for a period of time?

172. Which two Doctors appear in the episode *The Two Doctors*?

173. What does the Tardis *normally* look like?

174. Who do various villains lock in the Pandorica?

175. What was the trial season called for the sixth doctor?

176. In what year did Doctor Who first appear on TV?

177. What does Captain Jack use to travel through time when not with the Doctor?

178. What monster did the Doctor fight from the Himalayas?

179. What item of clothing is the fourth Doctor most famous for wearing?

180. Who fought against the Time Lords in the Time Wars?

# Monsters – Which Story? (3)

*Time once again to match the monster with their first story...*

181. Dalek

182. Vervoid

183. Voord

184. Nimon

185. Thal

186. Shakri

187. Marshman

188. Headless Monk

189. Siren

190. Pyrovile

# Who Played? (2)

*Which actor or actress played the following part..?*

191.  Susan Foreman

192.  Ben Jackson

193.  Adelaide Brooke

194.  Liz Shaw

195.  Wilfred Mott

196.  Vislor Turlough

197.  Polly

198.  Tegan Jovanka

199.  Melanie Bush

200.  Mickey Smith

# Monsters – Which Doctor? [3]

*Which brave Doctor faced the following..?*

201. Atraxi

202. Jagrafess

203. The Veil

204. Chimeron

205. Ganger

206. The Silence

207. Headless Monk

208. Scarecrow

209. Weeping Angel

210. Snowmen

# Planets (2)

*Guess the planet from the description...*

211. Home of a frog-like race, situated in the Inokshi System, in the Galaxy 1489.

212. The location of the Doomsday Weapon in Colony in Space.

213. Home planet of the Doctor's companion Turlough.

214. Home to the Candle Meadows and is the origin of Psychic Pollen.

215. The ultraviolet rays from this planet's sun makes its atmosphere poisonous to humans. It has four seasons, each lasting five hundred years.

216. The homeworld of Kane, the icy ruler of Iceworld.

217. The headquarters of the Issigri Mining Corporation.

218. The Lost breeding planet of the Adipose.

219. The most relaxing planet in the Galaxy.

220. The penal planet of the Terileptils.

# Stories – Which Doctor? (4)

*Which of the Doctors starred in these episodes or serials..?*

221. *Planet of the Daleks*

222. *Cold Blood*

223. *The Mind Robber*

224. *The Doctor Dances*

225. *The Romans*

226. *The Ambassadors of Death*

227. *Invasion of the Dinosaurs*

228. *The Talons of Weng-Chiang*

229. *Revenge of the Cybermen*

230. *Snakedance*

# Monster Anagrams (2)

*Jumbled up monster time! Decode the following...*

231. Welsh Tara

232. Six Groat

233. Wet Marsh

234. Soda Pie

235. I Tell Tripe

236. Aging Smog Tat

237. Sunny Rat

238. Falcon Tea

239. Ham Squad Tune

240. Die Knob

# Characters (2)

*Who are we describing here..?*

241. The designation of a shape-shifting alien resembling a giant viperfish in its natural form.

242. A sorceress from another dimension, who had previously battled Merlin.

243. A Saturnyne who flees the destruction of her planet along with her offspring.

244. A Daemon from the planet Daemos, who terrorises Devil's End.

245. Guardian of the Solar System in the year 4000 AD and a collaborator with the Daleks.

246. An entity that devoured life itself which, in the form of a humanoid skull, was buried under volcanic rock.

247. A cyborg, with half of his body covered in robotic prosthetics, and has a pet robot parrot, named Polyphase Avitron.

248. The Chief Executive of Ood Operations.

249. Masqueraded as an invited guest, Robina Redmond, in order to steal the Firestone from Lady Clemency Eddison.

250. The sadistic and despotic ruler of the planet Karfel.

# Pot Luck (5)

*No need for an introduction to these questions...*

251. What did Martha do for a job when she first met the Doctor?

252. What are the plastic beings called who came to kill the Doctor several times?

253. What was the spin-off series starring Sarah Jane called?

254. What are the names of the first two human companions to join the first Doctor?

255. From which Planet do the Cybermen originate?

256. What creature from the third moon of Delta Magna ingested a segment of the key to time?

257. Which companion is named after a well-known flower?

258. Who or what does Captain Jack become in the future?

259. What is Captain Jack's surname?

260. What is the eventual name of Amy and Rory's daughter?

# Stories – Which Doctor? (5)

*That time already?! Which Doctor starred in...*

261. *School Reunion*

262. *The Visitation*

263. *Flatline*

264. *Horror of Fang Rock*

265. *The Long Game*

266. *The Idiot's Lantern*

267. *Victory of the Daleks*

268. *The Empty Child*

269. *The Android Invasion*

270. *A Good Man Goes to War*

# Monsters – Which Doctor? (4)

*Also familiar now, who ran into these monsters...*

271. Siren

272. Quantum Shade

273. Judoon

274. Saturnyn

275. Castrovalvan

276. The Foretold

277. Krafayis

278. The Fisher King

279. Vinvocci

280. Boekind

# Companions (2)

*For those who have forgotten... of which Doctor were the following characters first companions?*

281.  Steven Taylor

282.  Harry Sullivan

283.  Sarah Jane Smith

284.  Brigadier Lethbridge-Stewart

285.  Jamie McCrimmon

286.  Ace

287.  Clara Oswald

288.  Amy Pond

289.  Jack Harkness

290.  Vislor Turlough

# Planets (3)

*Of the many worlds in the heavens, which one best fits the following descriptions...?*

291. A planet where dogs have no noses.

292. A frontier world where the character Milo Clancey has his base.

293. The seventh planet in the Dundra System in the Garn Belt.

294. A planet of Tau Ceti notable for its amino acid swamps.

295. Has golden spas, anti-gravity restaurants, sapphire waterfalls, and a landscape of diamonds.

296. Said to have a sky that looks like oil on water, and the place where you can see a burst of starfire.

297. The planet on which the Second Doctor encounters the Dominators.

298. A planet the Master promises to take his wife to that has whirlpools of gold.

299. A planet where the natives communicate with their eyebrows.

300. A swampy satellite of this planet is home to the vicious Drashigs.

# Monsters – Which Story? (4)

*Yet again, name the serial or episode in which we encounter...*

301. Cybermen (Mondasian)

302. Adipose

303. Krafayis

304. Toclafane

305. Giant Maggots

306. Peg Doll

307. Fenric

308. Malus

309. The Mire

310. The Teller

# Companions Introduced

*In which story were we introduced to the following companions..?*

311.  Jamie McCrimmon

312.  Harry Sullivan

313.  Adric

314.  Vislor Turlough

315.  Ace

316.  Rose Tyler

317.  Adam Mitchell

318.  Martha Jones

319.  Amy Pond

320.  Captain Jack Harkness

# Pot Luck (6)

*Pot luck time again!*

321. What are the cousins of the Silurians called?

322. What colours were the two Guardians in *The Key to Time*?

323. What town does Ace originally come from?

324. Who was the creator of the Daleks?

325. What is the name of the Doctor's wife?

326. Which enemy featured in the two Doctor Who cinema films?

327. Which actor appeared in the Doctor Who films *and* in the series – but as a different character?

328. What planet did the Cybermen take as their home after their original one was destroyed?

329. In which episode did the Doctor go up against some werewolves?

330. What was the spin off pilot featuring K9 called?

# Monsters – Which Story? (5)

*Another chance to guess the serial or episode in which we first came across these fantastic creatures...*

331. The Swarm

332. Chimeron

333. Vinvocci

334. Skovox Blitzer

335. Jagrafess

336. Abzorbaloff

337. Snowmen

338. Tharil

339. The Sandmen

340. Tivolians

# Planets (4)

*Time once more to guess the planet...*

341. Home planet of the Canisians.

342. The native creatures of this planet are the Screamers.

343. The location of the Singing Towers.

344. A planet rich in the rare mineral Oolion until it was destroyed by Zanak.

345. The location of Helen A's supposedly misery-free colony.

346. The farthest planet out in the known universe, which contains samples of anti-matter.

347. The homeworld of most of the Earth's bees.

348. A world famous for having the galaxy's largest flora collection.

349. This planet has mountains that sway in the breeze.

350. The home planet of the Abzorbaloff.

# Monsters – Which Doctor? (5)

*You should be getting used to this by now..!*

351. Zygon

352. Boneless

353. Ogron

354. Cyberman (Mondas)

355. Tharil

356. Thal

357. Skovox Blitzer

358. The Sandmen

359. Eternal

360. Terileptil

# Who Played? [3]

*Time to show your behind-the-scenes knowledge. Who played these companions..?*

361. Dodo Chaplet

362. Jamie McCrimmon

363. Barbara Wright

364. Jackson Lake

365. River Song

366. Jack Harkness

367. Astrid Peth

368. Harry Sullivan

369. Ace

370. Lady Christina de Souza

# Stories – Which Doctor? (6)

*The sixth installment of this subject: which Doctor starred in the following..?*

371. *The Curse of Fenric*

372. *The Highlanders*

373. *The Unquiet Dead*

374. *Terror of the Autons*

375. *Terror of the Zygons*

376. *The Space Pirates*

377. *The Pandorica Opens*

378. *The King's Demons*

379. *Four to Doomsday*

380. *Revelation of the Daleks*

# Pot Luck (7)

*More nuggets of information hopefully just within the grasp of your memory...*

381. Which companion appears to have died at the end of the episode *Earthshock*?

382. Which well-known comedienne also played a companion?

383. What enemy of the Doctor wears a full metal helmet?

384. During the time of the tenth Doctor, at what time of year did the Sycorax invade?

385. What creature does the Doctor go up against in *City of Death*?

386. Name the spin-off series whose title is an anagram of Doctor Who.

387. Who was the Runaway Bride?

388. In which episode did we first met Polly and Ben?

389. In which episode does the second Doctor meet Jamie?

390. Who will 'get you' if you blink?

# Monsters – Which Story? (6)

*You should know what to do by now...*

391.  The Wire

392.  Boneless

393.  Star Whale

394.  Ood

395.  Saturnyn

396.  Ganger

397.  Boekind

398.  Swampie

399.  Quantum Shade

400.  The Beast

# Characters (3)

*Which characters are being described here..?*

401. Accompanies Marco Polo on his caravan to Peking in 1289.

402. The mysterious manager of Satellite 5, an orbital news station around Earth broadcasting in 200,000.

403. This character's appearance resembles that of a huge red humanoid spider.

404. An anthropomorphic personification of the forces of entropy and chaos.

405. Leader of the monks who capture the Torchwood Estate and give refuge to a werewolf.

406. An ancient being that has been trapped for billions of years in a pit at the centre of the planet orbiting a black hole.

407. A ruthless Mexican-born politician who attempts to take control of the United Zones Organisation.

408. The possessor of a stolen Mark IV TARDIS with a fully functioning Chameleon Circuit.

409. A genius robotocist and partner of businessman Trau Morgus.

410. The finance-obsessed Usurian overlord of the humans on Pluto.

# Stories – Which Doctor? (7)

*Yet again, which Doctor featured prominently in these stories..?*

411. *Daleks in Manhattan*

412. *The Satan Pit*

413. *The Ice Warriors*

414. *Dragonfire*

415. *The Greatest Show in the Galaxy*

416. *The Monster of Peladon*

417. *Into the Dalek*

418. *Rise of the Cybermen*

419. *The Ark in Space*

420. *The Family of Blood*

# Monsters – Which Doctor? (6)

*And which Doctor encountered these wonderful aliens..?*

421.  Nimon

422.  Logopolitan

423.  The Mire

424.  Mara

425.  Stigorax

426.  Vigil

427.  Reaper

428.  Time Beetle

429.  Cheetah People

430.  Whisper Men

# Year of the Doctor

*Which Doctor was introduced to us in each of the following years..?*

431.  1981

432.  1966

433.  1984

434.  1963

435.  1974

436.  1970

437.  1996

438.  2013

439.  2010

440.  1987

# Pot Luck (8)

*The entire Whoniverse is explored in another round of pot luck...*

441. What is Amy's husband called?

442. On what planet is the 'Greatest Show in the Galaxy'?

443. What colour is the rare flower in the title of a fifth Doctor episode?

444. Under which doctor's tenure – and for a bonus point, in which episode – were we introduced to the Sonic Screwdriver?

445. What is the most likely thing you will hear someone say in a Dalek voice?

446. What colour is the Tardis?

447. What South American race does the first Doctor encounter?

448. What was used as a wearable alternative to the Sonic Screwdriver?

449. What was the Brigadier's full name ?

450. What did Sarah Jane do for a job when she first met the Doctor?

# Characters (4)

*One more time; who are we talking about here..?*

451. This character was elected as Lord Mayor of Cardiff and planned to leave Earth by using the energy from a new nuclear power station to interact with the Cardiff Rift.

452. The head of International Electromatics.

453. A physically disabled genius and megalomaniac, head of Cybus Industries on a parallel Earth.

454. Plans to destroy the world, at one point claiming (in a rather thick accent) "Nothing in the world can stop me now!"

455. A Knight of the nobility of the planet Tara and the Lord of Castle Gracht.

456. This character plans to take over the world with an army of snowmen.

457. A human physician and scientist of great renown, and a follower of the Time Lord tyrant Morbius.

458. An alias for Brother Lassar, the leader of a group of Krillitanes.

459. Leader of the Bannermen.

460. The gargoyle servant of the Dæmon from the planet Dæmos, who terrorises Devil's End.

# Monster Anagrams [3]

*Can you unscramble these aliens..?*

461. Alan Stomp

462. Lagoon Pilot

463. Tibet Melee

464. Soccer War

465. Insect Heel

466. Elk in Trial

467. Arson Ant

468. Vast Coral Van

469. Gherkin Fetish

470. Tat Carrot

# Stories – Which Doctor? (8)

*Some more serials and episodes for you... but which Doctor undertook the missions therein..?*

471. *Forest of the Dead*

472. *The Magician's Apprentice*

473. *The Mark of the Rani*

474. *The Vampires of Venice*

475. *Nightmare in Silver*

476. *The Happiness Patrol*

477. *The Power of Three*

478. *Dark Water*

479. *Asylum of the Daleks*

480. *Terminus*

# Monsters – Which Story? (7)

*And once again, in which episode or serial did we first meet these..?*

481. Ice Warrior

482. Isolus

483. Ogron

484. Cheetah People

485. Hath

486. Terileptil

487. Vespiform

488. Time Beetle

489. Stigorax

490. Judoon

# Who Played? (4)

*The title says it all..!*

491. Adric

492. Vicki

493. Leela

494. Victoria Waterfield

495. Adam Mitchell

496. Martha Jones

497. Romana

498. Ian Chesterton

499. Clara Oswald

500. Craig Owens

# Monsters – Which Doctor? (7)

*Some more creatures that you'll surely remember; but which Doctor can recall being the first to encouter them?*

501.  Pyrovile

502.  Star Whale

503.  Vervoid

504.  The Swarm

505.  Plasmaton

506.  Krillitane

507.  Swampie

508.  Gelth

509.  Abzorbaloff

510.  Time Zombie

# Pot Luck (9)

*Almost there... the penultimate pot luck pickings!*

511. Who was the female Time Lord that tried to beat the Doctor?

512. What sort of metal is the living statue made of in 'Silver Nemesis'?

513. What is the name of the girl who claims to be the Doctor's daughter?

514. In which city does the Eighth Doctor's TV Movie take place?

515. What does the acronym TARDIS stand for?

516. What is the name of the village in the episode *The Daemons*?

517. What is the alias the Doctor often uses?

518. What does UNIT stand for?

519. Which monsters try to turn the Empire State building into a giant antenna?

520. In what episode was the aircraft Concorde featured?

# Planets (5)

*Your last chance to determine which alien worlds are being described here...*

521. A planet where the continental land mass is shaped like a lamenting woman.

522. The planetary home of the Hop Pyleen brothers, inventors of Hyposlip Travel Systems.

523. A jungle-covered world inhabited by the Mechonoids.

524. Grant Markham's home world.

525. The lost moon of this planet was the subject of study by student Dee Dee Blasco.

526. Home to a human-like race, the disembodied brains of Morpho, and the Voord.

527. The home of Chantho's people, the Malmooth.

528. A planet promised to Luke Rattigan by the Sontarans.

529. A planet impossibly in orbit around a black hole.

530. A frozen planet used as a final resting place for the galaxy's dead.

# Stories – Which Doctor? (9)

*From the first to the twelfth, which Doctor starred in these stories..?*

531. *The Keeper of Traken*

532. *The Caretaker*

533. *Blink*

534. *The Mysterious Planet*

535. *Doctor Who and the Silurians*

536. *Fury from the Deep*

537. *Attack of the Cybermen*

538. *The Masque of Mandragora*

539. *Tooth and Claw*

540. *The Rebel Flesh*

# Anagram Companions (2)

*Which companions have had their letters scrambled here..?*

541.  Bright Arab War

542.  Oh Cold Adept

543.  Cash Jerk Sank

544.  London Bean

545.  Joan Hamster

546.  Dirt Met Fowl

547.  Her Zoo Tie

548.  Sir Govern

549.  Leery Sort

550.  Anita Ark

# Monsters – Which Doctor? (8)

*For the final time, which Doctor first encountered the following monsters..?*

551. Ice Warrior

552. Rutan

553. Auton

554. Aridian

555. Sisterhood of Karn

556. Sontaran

557. Vespiform

558. Marshman

559. Great Intelligence

560. Silurian

# Monsters – Which Story? (8)

*And a last chance to determine the story that introduced us to...*

561. Scarecrow

562. Reaper

563. Sycorax

564. Weeping Angel

565. Sontaran

566. The Foretold

567. Raxacoricofallapatorian

568. Aridian

569. Zygon

570. Plasmaton

# Monster Anagrams (4)

*Can you unscramble these well-known but jumbled-up aliens?*

571. US Soil

572. Criterion A

573. Seldom Shaken

574. Liar in Us

575. Negligee Pawn

576. No Judo E

577. A Coaxial Polaron Aircraft

578. Acorn and I

579. Ask Fairy

580. Micro Hen

# Stories – Which Doctor? (10)

*One final batch of stories. Which Doctor starred in..?*

581. *The Mutants*

582. *The Creature from the Pit*

583. *Evolution of the Daleks*

584. *Ghost Light*

585. *The Fires of Pompeii*

586. *The Armageddon Factor*

587. *Delta and the Bannermen*

588. *Face the Raven*

589. *Underworld*

590. *The Androids of Tara*

# Pot Luck (10)

*Well done, you've made it to the end! Now a nice little mixture to finish things off with...*

591. Which famous female singer starred in the episode *Voyage of the Damned*?

592. What shape was on the end of the Seventh Doctor's umbrella?

593. What was the Doctor's car called?

594. What creatures control the Loch Ness Monster?

595. Where in his body is K9's laser?

596. Travelling with the eleventh Doctor is a female companion called Amy; but what is her surname?

597. Which famous UK athlete has a street named after her in Doctor Who?

598. What is the fourth Doctor's favourite sweet?

599. Which famous writer does the Doctor meet in the episode *The Unicorn and the Wasp*?

600. What was the name of the Doctor's notably Scottish companion?

# The Answers

# Stories – Which Doctor? (1)

1. Tenth

2. First

3. Second

4. Third

5. Fourth

6. Eleventh

7. Fifth

8. Second

9. First

10. Eleventh

# Monsters – Which Doctor? (1)

11. Seventh

12. Tenth

13. First

14. Tenth

15. Tenth

16. Tenth

17. Fifth

18. Third

19. Tenth

20. Tenth

# Monsters – Which Story? (1)

# Pot Luck (1)

31. The Sycorax

32. The Whomobile

33. Mel

34. Metebelis Three

35. Shada

36. Fenric

37. William Hartnell, Patrick Troughton, Jon Pertwee, Tom Baker, Peter Davison, Colin Baker, Sylvester McCoy, Paul McGann, Christopher Eccleston, David Tennant, Matt Smith, Peter Capaldi

38. The Cybermen

39. K9

40. The Weeping Angels

# Planets (1)

41.   Kolkokron (or Culkacron)

42.   Chimeria

43.   Riftan Five

44.   Skaar

45.   Pen Haxico 2

46.   Arkannis Major

47.   Kataa Floko

48.   Karas don Kazra don Slava

49.   Varos

50.   Qualactin

# Anagram Companions (1)

51. Ben Jackson

52. Liz Shaw

53. Jo Grant

54. Leela

55. Romana

56. Adric

57. Nyssa

58. Amy Pond

59. Ace

60. Peri Brown

# Stories – Which Doctor? (2)

61. First

62. First

63. Sixth

64. Fourth

65. Third

66. Ninth

67. Tenth

68. Second

69. Fifth

70. First

# Monsters – Which Doctor? (2)

71.  Ninth

72.  First

73.  Tenth

74.  Eleventh

75.  Fifth

76.  Eleventh

77.  Third

78.  Fifth

79.  Seventh

80.  Tenth

# Pot Luck (2)

81. Torchwood

82. The Meddling Monk

83. The Silurians

84. Twelve

85. Susan

86. Ace

87. A junk yard

88. Dodo

89. UNIT

90. Alex Kingston

# Characters (1)

91.   Yvonne Hartman

92.   The Celestial Toymaker

93.   WOTAN

94.   Caven

95.   Borusa

96.   Kroagnon (or The Great Architect)

97.   Harrison Chase

98.   Megron

99.   De Flores

100.   Helen A

# Monster Anagrams (1)

101. Siren

102. Mandrel

103. Atraxi

104. Rutan

105. Auton

106. Swampie

107. Cryon

108. Thal

109. Cyberman

110. Sycorax

# Who Played? [1]

111. John Levene

112. Elisabeth Sladen

113. Wendy Padbury

114. Arthur Darvill

115. Catherine Tate

116. Peter Purves

117. Nicola Bryant

118. Richard Franklin

119. Billie Piper

120. Katy Manning

# Monsters – Which Story? (2)

121. *School Reunion*

122. *Frontios*

123. *Heaven Sent*

124. *The Unquiet Dead*

125. *The Brain of Morbius*

126. *Logopolis*

127. *The Happiness Patrol*

128. *The Name of the Doctor*

129. *The Web Planet*

130. *The Rings of Akhaten*

# Pot Luck (3)

131. The Macra

132. Skaro

133. Peter Purves

134. The chameleon circuit

135. Five

136. Raxacoricofallapatorius

137. The Master

138. *Remembrance of the Daleks*

139. Grant

140. Van Gogh

# Which Doctor

141. First

142. Ninth

143. Third

144. Fifth

145. Tenth

146. Eighth

147. Sixth

148. Second

149. Fouth

150. Seventh

# Companions (1)

151. Fourth

152. Eigth

153. First

154. Eleventh

155. Ninth

156. Tenth

157. First

158. Sixth

159. Third

160. Fourth

# Stories – Which Doctor? (3)

161.  First

162.  Eleventh

163.  Tenth

164.  Fourth

165.  Second

166.  Third

167.  First

168.  Seventh

169.  First

170.  Fourth

# Pot Luck (4)

171. Kamelion

172. The second and the sixth Doctors

173. A police telephone box

174. The Doctor

175. Trial of a Time Lord

176. 1963

177. A Vortex Manipulator

178. The Yeti

179. A very long scarf

180. The Daleks

# Monsters – Which Story? (3)

181. *The Daleks*

182. *Terror of the Vervoids*

183. *The Sea of Death*

184. *The Horns of Nimon*

185. *The Daleks*

186. *The Power of Three*

187. *Full Circle*

188. *A Good Man Goes to War*

189. *The Curse of the Black Spot*

190. *The Fires of Pompeii*

# Who Played? (2)

191. Carole Ann Ford

192. Michael Craze

193. Lindsay Duncan

194. Caroline John

195. Bernard Cribbins

196. Mark Strickson

197. Anneke Wills

198. Janet Fielding

199. Bonnie Langford

200. Noel Clarke

# Monsters – Which Doctor? [3]

201. Eleventh

202. Ninth

203. Twelfth

204. Seventh

205. Eleventh

206. Eleventh

207. Eleventh

208. Tenth

209. Tenth

210. Eleventh

# Planets (2)

211. Urbanka

212. Uxarieus

213. Trion

214. Karass Don Slava

215. Solos

216. Proamon

217. Ta

218. Adipose 3

219. Diadem

220. Raaga

# Stories – Which Doctor? (4)

221. Third

222. Eleventh

223. Second

224. Ninth

225. First

226. Third

227. Third

228. Fourth

229. Fourth

230. Fifth

# Monster Anagrams (2)

231. Star Whale

232. Stigorax

233. The Swarm

234. Adipose

235. Terileptil

236. Giant Maggots

237. Saturnyn

238. Toclafane

239. Quantum Shade

240. Boekind

# Characters (2)

241. Prisoner Zero

242. Morgaine

243. Signora Rosanna Calvierri

244. Azal

245. Mavic Chen

246. The Fendahl

247. The Captain

248. Klineman Halpen

249. The Unicorn

250. The Borad

# Pot Luck (5)

# Stories – Which Doctor? (5)

261.  Tenth

262.  Fifth

263.  Twelfth

264.  Fourth

265.  Ninth

266.  Tenth

267.  Eleventh

268.  Ninth

269.  Fourth

270.  Eleventh

# Monsters – Which Doctor? (4)

271. Eleventh

272. Twelfth

273. Tenth

274. Eleventh

275. Fifth

276. Twelfth

277. Eleventh

278. Twelfth

279. Tenth

280. Ninth

# Companions (2)

281. First

282. Fourth

283. Third

284. Second

285. Second

286. Seventh

287. Eleventh

288. Eleventh

289. Ninth

290. Fifth

# Planets (3)

291. Barcelona

292. Lobos

293. Alfava Metraxis

294. Ogros

295. Midnight

296. Meta Sigmafolio

297. Dulkis

298. Catrigan Nova

299. Delphon

300. Grundle

# Monsters – Which Story? (4)

# Companions Introduced

311. *The Highlanders*

312. *Robot*

313. *Full Circle*

314. *Mawdryn Undead*

315. *Dragonfire*

316. *Rose*

317. *Dalek*

318. *Smith and Jones*

319. *The Eleventh Hour*

320. *The Empty Child*

# Pot Luck (6)

321. The Sea Devils

322. Black and White

323. Perivale

324. Davros

325. River Song

326. The Daleks

327. Bernard Cribbins

328. Telos

329. *Tooth and Claw*

330. K9 and company

# Monsters – Which Story? (5)

# Planets (4)

341. Alpha Canis One (or Canis Major)

342. Desperus

343. Darillium

344. Bandraginus 5

345. Terra Alpha

346. Zeta Minor

347. Melissa Majoria

348. Zaakros

349. Felspoon

350. Clom

# Monsters – Which Doctor? (5)

351. Fourth

352. Twelfth

353. Third

354. First

355. Fourth

356. First

357. Twelfth

358. Twelfth

359. Fifth

360. Fifth

# Who Played? [3]

361. Jackie Lane

362. Frazer Hines

363. Jacqueline Hill

364. David Morrissey

365. Alex Kingston

366. John Barrowman

367. Kylie Minogue

368. Ian Marter

369. Sophie Aldred

370. Michelle Ryan

# Stories – Which Doctor? (6)

371. Seventh

372. Second

373. Ninth

374. Third

375. Fourth

376. Second

377. Eleventh

378. Fifth

379. Fifth

380. Sixth

# Pot Luck (7)

381. Adric

382. Catherine Tate

383. The Sontarans

384. Christmas

385. Scaroth

386. Torchwood

387. Donna Noble

388. *The War Machines*

389. *The Highlanders*

390. A Weeping Angel

# Monsters – Which Story? (6)

391. *The Idiot's Lantern*

392. *Flatline*

393. *The Beast Below*

394. *The Impossible Planet*

395. *The Vampires of Venice*

396. *The Rebel Flesh*

397. *The End of the World*

398. *The Power of Kroll*

399. *Face the Raven*

400. *The Satan Pit*

# Characters (3)

401. Tegana

402. The Editor

403. The Empress of the Racnoss

404. The Black Guardian

405. Father Angelo

406. The Beast

407. Ramón Salamander

408. The Meddling Monk

409. Sharaz Jek

410. The Collector

# Stories – Which Doctor? (7)

411. Tenth

412. Tenth

413. Second

414. Seventh

415. Seventh

416. Third

417. Twelfth

418. Tenth

419. Fourth

420. Tenth

# Monsters – Which Doctor? (6)

421. Fourth

422. Fourth

423. Twelfth

424. Fifth

425. Seventh

426. Eleventh

427. Ninth

428. Tenth

429. Seventh

430. Eleventh

# Year of the Doctor

431. Fifth

432. Second

433. Sixth

434. First

435. Fourth

436. Third

437. Eighth

438. Twelfth

439. Eleventh

440. Seventh

# Pot Luck (8)

441. Rory Williams

442. Segona

443. Black Orchid

444. The Second Doctor: Fury From the Deep

445. Exterminate!

446. Blue

447. The Aztec's

448. A pair of Ray-Ban sunglasses

449. Brigadier Alistair Gordon Lethbridge-Stewart

450. Reporter

# Characters (4)

# Monster Anagrams (3)

461. Plasmaton

462. Logopolitan

463. Time Beetle

464. Scarecrow

465. The Silence

466. Krillitane

467. Sontaran

468. Castrovalvan

469. The Fisher King

470. Tractator

# Stories – Which Doctor? (8)

471. Tenth

472. Twelfth

473. Sixth

474. Eleventh

475. Eleventh

476. Seventh

477. Eleventh

478. Twelfth

479. Eleventh

480. Fifth

# Monsters – Which Story? (7)

481. *The Ice Warriors*

482. *Fear Her*

483. *Day of the Daleks*

484. *Survival*

485. *The Doctor's Daughter*

486. *The Visitation*

487. *The Unicorn and the Wasp*

488. *Turn Left*

489. *The Happiness Patrol*

490. *Smith and Jones*

# Who Played? (4)

491. Matthew Waterhouse

492. Maureen O'Brien

493. Louise Jameson

494. Deborah Watling

495. Bruno Langley

496. Freema Agyeman

497. Mary Tamm

498. William Russell

499. Jenna Coleman

500. James Corden

# Monsters – Which Doctor? (7)

501. Tenth

502. Eleventh

503. Sixth

504. Tenth

505. Fifth

506. Tenth

507. Fourth

508. Ninth

509. Tenth

510. Eleventh

# Pot Luck (9)

# Planets [5]

521. Woman Wept

522. Rex Vox Jax

523. Mechanus

524. Agora

525. Poosh

526. Marinus

527. Malcassairo

528. Castor 36

529. Krop Tor

530. Necros

# Stories – Which Doctor? (9)

531. Fourth

532. Twelfth

533. Tenth

534. Sixth

535. Third

536. Second

537. Sixth

538. Fourth

539. Tenth

540. Eleventh

# Anagram Companions (2)

541. Barbara Wright

542. Dodo Chaplet

543. Jack Harkness

544. Donna Noble

545. Martha Jones

546. Wilfred Mott

547. Zoe Heriot

548. River Song

549. Rose Tyler

550. Katarina

551. Second

552. Fourth

553. Third

554. First

555. Fourth

556. Third

557. Tenth

558. Fourth

559. Second

560. Third

# Monsters – Which Story? (8)

561. *Human Nature*

562. *Father's Day*

563. *The Christmas Invasion*

564. *Blink*

565. *The Time Warrior*

566. *Mummy on the Orient Express*

567. *Aliens of London*

568. *The Executioners*

569. *Terror of the Zygons*

570. *Time-Flight*

# Monster Anagrams (4)

571. Isolus

572. Carrionite

573. Headless Monk

574. Silurian

575. Weeping Angel

576. Judoon

577. Raxacoricofallapatorian

578. Draconian

579. Krafayis

580. Chimeron

# Stories – Which Doctor? (10)

581. Third

582. Fourth

583. Tenth

584. Seventh

585. Tenth

586. Fourth

587. Seventh

588. Twelfth

589. Fourth

590. Fourth

# Pot Luck (10)

591. Kylie Minogue

592. A Question mark

593. Bessie

594. The Zygons

595. Nose

596. Pond

597. Dame Kelly Holmes

598. Jelly Babies

599. Agatha Christie

600. Jamie

You may also enjoy...